DETROIT PUBLIC LIBRARY
3 5674 00965695 1

W9-CAB-496

THE CLOUD SHOES

ALSO BY BORGHILD DAHL

GLIMPSES OF NORWAY

I WANTED TO SEE

KAREN

HOMECOMING

THE DAUGHTER

The Cloud Shoes

BY BORGHILD DAHL

Illustrated by Hans Helweg

E. P. DUTTON & CO., INC. · NEW YORK

FIRST PRINTING SEPTEMBER 1957
SECOND PRINTING MARCH 1962

Library of Congress Catalog Card Number: 57-8979

To

James Ramsey Tamarelli

and

Robert Bruce Tamarelli

THE CLOUD SHOES

Long ago in old Norway when, it is said, there were more trolls and elves than there were human beings, the whole country was divided into small kingdoms. Over one of these ruled a wise and good king named Brynne. His kingdom was called Brynnedalen, meaning the valley of Brynne, but in time this was changed to Brydalen because it was easier to say.

King Brynne ruled his people from an ice palace on a mountaintop. Every time a stranger came to Brydalen, the people down in the valley would point up to the highest tower above which floated King Brynne's white flag with its gold crown encircled by a crimson wreath. And they would exclaim, "Look, stranger! Up there dwells our beloved King. His palace was once a jewel in the crown of the great god Odin, when he ruled over other gods at Valhalla." The stranger would be sure to cry out in wonder and admiration at what he saw.

Only the rulers of the neighboring kingdoms failed to praise the ice palace. This was because they were envious of King Brynne, and the sight of his ice palace, blazing with lights, reminded them of his greatness. They were also jealous of Queen Edel, who was as kind as she was beautiful. As for Prince Melchior, the only child of King Brynne and Queen Edel — so handsome and clever was he — he might have been a great-great-grandson of the god Odin himself.

Although King Brynne and Queen Edel and Prince Melchior lived on the mountaintop, scarcely a day passed when all three of them were not to be seen down in the valley. King Brynne went out into the fields with the men and showed them how to hang the hay on poles so it would dry, and how to cut and shock grain. For the kingdom of Brydalen lay so far north that the winters were long and cold and the growing season short. And it was therefore very important to attend to the crops while the warm weather lasted.

Queen Edel, though small and dainty, worked with the farmers' wives. With her fur crown on her head, she showed them how to make clothes from the skins of the animals that the men had brought home from the hunt. And she cooked delicious food and told the women and girls exactly how it was done, so that they could serve the same tasty dishes to their families.

Prince Melchior seemed to be everywhere at once. While the men were out in the fields down in the valley, he carried drinking water for them and brought their food to them when they were too busy to go to their homes. Up on the mountains, when the women and older girls were in the chalets, he ran errands and fed the cattle and went in search of lost sheep. And whenever the younger children found their tasks particularly difficult, Prince Melchior was sure to be on hand to help them.

"If our children were all like Prince Melchior," the parents told one another, "Brydalen would some day become a great kingdom."

One spring the snow stayed down in the valley longer than usual. The sky remained overcast with gray clouds, and there was no sunshine. The farmers were late in plowing their fields. And after the grain had been planted, there was no rain to make it grow.

King Brynne went from one farm to another. "As you already see," he told the people on each place, "the grain crop will be miserably poor. Therefore, it will be necessary to make the most of every blade of grass in the kingdom."

The men and older boys combed the meadows down in the valley until they were bare. The women and the girls and the younger boys, Prince Melchior among them, went up into the mountain chalets and stayed there until late in the fall when the first snowflakes began to appear. The boys herded the cattle upon rocky ledges where no one had bothered to go for pasturage before. And the women and girls made cheese and butter out of every drop of milk. Yet when winter set in — much earlier than in other years — there was little to show for the hard work. The haymows were half empty. It was worse with the granaries. The cattle were scrawny, and the small chunks of butter and cheese in the storehouses could not possibly last until spring.

King Brynne called his wise men together in the state chamber of the ice palace. "I fear a famine," he told them. "Has anyone something to suggest which might help to prevent one?"

The wise men shook their heads.

King Brynne rose from his high seat. "Then hear me," he commanded. "Send out fishing parties at once. Every man and boy old enough to hold a fishing line or a net must go. Prince Melchior and I will go, too. When we return with our catches, the women and older girls must be on hand to salt and dry the fish. We must make haste before the rivers and lakes freeze over."

All the fishermen did their best. They laid out nets along the banks of the rivers and close to the shores of the lakes. They sat for days waiting for nibbles. And they waded out in the streams, hoping to seize the fish with their bare hands. As it grew colder, they had to chop holes in the ice and cast their lines and lay their nets in deep water. But either the fish sensed the attack that was being made on them, or had left Brydalen for warmer quarters. When the fishing parties finally gave up and returned with their meager catches, there was not, among them all, enough fish, when dried and salted, to feed one good-sized family over the winter.

King Brynne and Queen Edel visited every home. "Eat as sparingly of bread and butter and cheese and fish as possible," they begged the people. The grownups obeyed King Brynne and Queen Edel and the children tried to, but in spite of their best efforts, the food disappeared with alarming speed.

One afternoon when they were alone in their private chamber in the ice palace, King Brynne and Queen Edel talked over the plight of their people.

"Where will this end?" King Brynne asked, greatly worried.

"It may not be as bad as we fear," Queen Edel said, trying to appear calm. "With the winter well upon us, there should be good hunting."

Again King Brynne sat with his wise men in the state chamber of the ice palace. "If we bag enough game," he told them, "all may yet be well. This time let us go in one large party. Have every able-bodied man and boy ready for the hunt early in the morning. Prince Melchior and I will also go."

The moon was barely visible behind heavy clouds and the mountaintops looked gray and forbidding when the men and boys set out the following day. They climbed dangerously steep cliffs and followed trails into deep caverns. But although they did not give up until far into the night, they had nothing to show for their pains but a savage stringy bear that it had taken four men to kill.

"Roll into your sleeping bags," King Brynne commanded after the evening meal around the fire. "We are sure to have better luck in the morning."

But King Brynne did not sleep. A terrible fear gripped his heart. If the hunting, too, failed, what would become of his people? Could it be that an evil troll was enchanting the fish in the streams and the animals in the woods?

Suddenly King Brynne felt something wet strike his face. There was more and more of it. Soon his eyebrows and beard were covered with a thick layer of snow. He got out of his sleeping bag and stood up stiffly.

The others woke up, too. Prince Melchior rubbed his eyes sleepily.

"Perhaps the prince should not have come along," one hunter said, real concern in his voice. "He is younger than all the rest and —"

"Prince Melchior can weather a storm as well as any of us," King Brynne interrupted brusquely.

As the hunters started for home, the snow fell faster and faster. It covered the tracks of animals and it filled the path over which the hunters had traveled the day before. They had difficulty finding the way. When they finally dragged themselves into Brydalen, they were too tired to care whether they had bagged any game or not. But King Brynne, true to his promise, blew his horn as a signal of their return.

The women were overjoyed to see them. "You were wise to come home when it stormed," they said happily. "We can eat well for a long time on the game that you have brought. Have but a little patience and the fresh meat will be sizzling in pots over our fires."

The hunters kept their eyes fixed on the ground. King Brynne looked over at Queen Edel pleadingly, and she understood.

"Our men have had bad luck," she told the women quietly.

"Take your children into your homes and give them warm porridge."

It was with a heavy heart that King Brynne trudged beside Queen Edel and Prince Melchior up the mountain to their ice palace. The higher they went, the worse grew the storm, and the wind almost blew them down into the valley again before the great door had closed behind them.

On the fifth day of the storm, King Brynne and Queen Edel sat in their high seats in the state chamber. Prince Melchior lay on a rug of otter skins before the gray hearth. A single candle sputtered feebly, throwing a dim light into the room.

"The storm is truly terrible," Queen Edel said. "I wonder how things are with our people down in the valley. I fear for them — especially the children."

"I would give anything I possess to help them," King Brynne said sadly.

Suddenly Prince Melchior jumped up from the rug. "Father," he cried, "what was that? Someone is at the door."

"It is only the storm," King Brynne assured him.

"Someone is knocking," Prince Melchior insisted.

Queen Edel slipped down from her high seat. "I think I do hear something," she admitted.

All three listened. For a few minutes everything was still. Then came three taps. They were gentle, yet so distinct that they could not possibly be mistaken for something else.

King Brynne stepped down from his high seat and walked across the room. Seizing the door knob, he pulled open the great door, creaking and groaning on its silver hinges. A gust of wind blew out the solitary candle. The tiny fire on the hearth died out, too, leaving the room in total darkness. Never since King Brynne and Queen Edel and Prince Melchior had come to live in the palace, had such a thing happened before.

"Who is there?" King Brynne demanded.

"It is I, a friend from Trond Mountain."

"I have no friend on Trond Mountain," King Brynne said, trying to make his voice sound natural. "But you are welcome nevertheless, be you a troll, an elf, or a human being. It shall not be said of King Brynne that he turned away a living creature on a night like this."

A low chuckle sounded out of the darkness. "I thank you," the voice said. "But now we must have some light."

There was a rustling sound as of dry leaves falling. Then the place was flooded with such dazzling light that, for a moment, King Brynne and Queen Edel and Prince Melchior were blinded. When they were able to see once more, they were amazed to find that a brisk fire was burning on the hearth, and that everything in the room — including ceiling, walls, floor, and furniture — sparkled as if set with millions of diamonds.

"That's better. It seems to me, King Brynne, that you have been a trifle neglectful of your lights."

King Brynne and Queen Edel exchanged glances. They were too proud to admit how low their supply of candles had become. Besides, they were too much surprised and too interested in the strange visitor to mind his gentle rebuke.

He stood perched on the very top of King Brynne's high seat, his small feet resting on the ice carving. He could not possibly have been more than two feet tall. He wore a green jacket and reddish-brown trousers, so covered with patches of every color of the rainbow that, on first sight, he looked like a huge bouquet of wild mountain flowers. Under his red peaked cap, his blue eyes sparkled like stars on a frosty night.

King Brynne and Queen Edel and Prince Melchior had always known that there must be plenty of trolls and elves in Brydalen, as there were in all other kingdoms of Norway. But this was their first experience meeting one face to face, and, for a minute, all three stood speechless.

Queen Edel was the first to recover. "If it is not considered bad manners among you elves," she said, "may I ask you what errand brings you into our kingdom?"

"I shall be glad to answer your question," the elf said smiling. "My errand in Brydalen tonight is to take advantage of King Brynne's generous offer. It was with great joy that I heard him say, only a few minutes ago, that he would be willing to give up anything he possessed, if by doing so he could end the famine among his people."

"I stand ready to make good that promise," King Brynne said promptly.

"Name what it is you wish, in order that we may have it brought to you at once," Queen Edel said. "As you know, our people are in great need of food."

The elf fixed his gaze first upon Queen Edel, and then he turned to King Brynne. "If I should ask you to give up your ice palace, would you be willing to make the sacrifice?"

"I would," King Brynne answered without the slightest hesitation.

Queen Edel nodded approval.

The elf smiled. "I shall not ask you to give up your ice palace," he said.

King Brynne and Queen Edel breathed more easily.

The elf leaned forward. "If," he said, "I should ask you to give up your crown, King Brynne, what then?"

King Brynne looked startled. But he recovered almost immediately and spoke in a firm voice. "To save my starving people, I would gladly give up my crown."

Again the elf smiled. "You may keep your crown," he said.

King Brynne and Queen Edel stood tense.

The elf leaned forward a little farther, and speaking more slowly than before, he asked: "In order to save your people from starvation, King Brynne, would you, if I should ask it of you, be willing to give up – Prince Melchior?"

"Our son?" King Brynne exclaimed in a strained voice. "What could you want with him?"

"He is only a child," Queen Edel said. "He needs the care of a father and mother. Besides, you would find him a great deal of trouble."

"You mean you are not willing to give him up?" the elf asked sharply. "I feared as much. You humans make promises so easily, but find it so hard to keep them."

He moved as if to hop down from his perch. "There is no further need for me to stay here discussing with you the hunger of your people," he said.

"Wait!" It was King Brynne who spoke. "Your request has taken us completely by surprise. We ask that you grant us time to think the matter over."

The elf stood upright and took a few tiny steps toward the top of King Brynne's high seat. "Very well," he said. "But make haste. I must be on my way."

King Brynne drew Queen Edel aside to their private chamber.

"You are his mother. It is for you to decide," King Brynne said brokenly.

"You are his father," Queen Edel said, kissing him. "We both love him equally as much."

"To save our starving people, it is necessary for us to act at once. Therefore, were I to speak for myself, I should have to say that my duty to them comes first."

"I speak for both of us then, when I say that our duty to our people must come first," Queen Edel said softly.

King Brynne embraced Queen Edel tenderly. "Let us have no fear for the safety of our son," he said.

"I cannot believe that any harm can come to him," Queen Edel agreed. "We are sending him on an errand of mercy. But we shall miss him sorely."

When King Brynne and Queen Edel returned to the state chamber, the elf regarded them expectantly. They walked over to King Brynne's high seat.

"We have made our decision," King Brynne said.

"And it is — ?"

"We will give up our son."

"You will remember that he has never before been away from home," Queen Edel said anxiously. "He is unused to the ways of the world."

"That I will," the elf promised.

"And you will wait long enough for me to find his warmest clothes?" Queen Edel asked. "It is a bitter night for a child to start out on a journey."

"I will wait," the elf said.

When Prince Melchior returned to the state chamber, he was so weighed down with furs that he could scarcely walk. Queen Edel followed close behind him, carrying a robe of silver fox skins, which she handed to the elf. King Brynne's eyes opened wide with astonishment as the tiny figure took the heavy robe and lifted it as easily as if it had been a feather.

"I'll take this along," the elf said smiling, "though you need have no fear that your son will suffer from the cold while he is with me. And now," he went on, assuming a very businesslike air, "for that other matter which we must settle immediately."

King Brynne and Queen Edel regarded the little man anxiously.

"In the southern kingdoms of Norway," the elf said, "there is no famine. Storehouses are full. People there can spare enough of everything to feed the entire kingdom of Brydalen."

"How can that help us?" Queen Edel asked. "This storm has buried the mountain peaks and filled the valleys with ice and snow. It will be months before anyone can travel so far, and then it will be too late."

"I have taken care of that," the elf told her. "Come out into the courtyard with me."

Before King Brynne and Queen Edel and Prince Melchior realized what was happening, the great door of the ice palace had swung wide open and the elf was standing outside perched on a high snowdrift. The wind had calmed down considerably, but there was still snow in the air.

"Do you see those?" the elf asked.

There were two long boards standing on end against the wall of the ice palace. Fastened to the middle of each was a leather thong. The upper ends of the boards had been whittled to sharp points that curved upward like the prows of Viking ships.

"These are magic shoes," the elf said. "Put them on your feet, King Brynne, and wear them on your journey to the Southland. There is no drift so deep, no mountain so high, and no kingdom so far away, but that the magic shoes will carry you there safely and quickly. And these," he said, hopping down from the snowdrift and landing on some sacks, "are full of gold. You will find it useful while bargaining with the farmers in the Southland."

"Thank you," King Brynne said.

"Now, before we part, I have a few words of advice to give you. If you will remember them and follow them, you will find them very useful on your journey. In low places, use your feet. In high places, use your head."

"I shall remember," King Brynne said respectfully. But to himself he thought, though of what use such strange advice can be, is beyond me.

Before King Brynne had had time to step over to the wall of the ice palace, against which the magic shoes rested, a sudden blast of wind almost swept him off his feet. At the same instant every light in the palace went out.

King Brynne looked about wildly. All he could see was Queen Edel, who stood close behind him. "My son!" he cried out in a horrified voice. "Wait, Elf!"

But there was no answer except the roar of the wind over the mountaintop.

"Oh, what have I done, what have I done?" King Brynne cried, the tears streaming down his cheeks and into his beard.

Queen Edel grasped his arm and raised her voice so it could be heard above the wind. "It will be all right!" she said. "Our only thought now must be of our starving people. Put the magic shoes on your feet and the sacks of gold on your back. I will go into the kitchen and prepare food for you to eat on your way."

King Brynne was still struggling with the magic shoes when Queen Edel returned, carrying a huge bundle. She fastened this and the sacks of gold on King Brynne's back, and pulled his feet into place under the leather thongs of the magic shoes. Then she kissed him good-by, and watched him set off on his journey.

King Brynne did not risk a backward glance. His heart was too full of sadness at what he had done. Moreover he had taken only a few steps when it came to him what a difficult struggle he had been plunged into. All paths had disappeared under the deep snow. The narrow shoes kept crossing in front of him so that he stumbled with every step. And each time he stumbled, he was almost smothered in snow.

After a dozen such tumbles, he became greatly disheartened. "I'll take these terrible things off my feet," he said savagely, doubling over and tugging at the thongs of one of the magic shoes.

Immediately the wind roared with such fury and beat the snow so hard against his face that he felt as though he had been pushed under a waterfall. Breathless and frightened, he dropped the thong and tried to stand upright.

It may have been his imagination, but it seemed to King Brynne that the storm calmed down considerably. And although his heart was heavy, he was moving forward, even though he had to force himself to lift each foot for every step he took.

Suddenly his legs gave way under him and he was lying flat on his back. There was cold snow in his eyes, ears, nose, and mouth. When he tried to move his feet, he found that they were hopelessly entangled in the wooden shoes. He sat up and put his hand to his head. It was bare except for more snow that was matted in his thick, curly hair. He looked anxiously around and there was his fur crown, lying on the ground a short distance away. Heavy with jewels and snow, it had fallen off. Half crawling, half sliding, he worked his way over to his crown. He picked it up, brushed off the snow, and placed it carefully back on his head.

"It is well that no one but Queen Edel saw me leave the ice palace," he whispered. "Otherwise, my people might have been out to wish me godspeed on my journey. And it would never do to have them see their king in such a position!"

It was with considerable difficulty that he disentangled himself from the wooden shoes and put them on properly. He stood up and regarded his surroundings. As far as he could see, nothing but the barren white waste stretched out before him. King Brynne wrung his hands.

"I shall never be able to reach the Southland on these miserable wooden shoes," he moaned. "I may as well go back before it is too late."

Slowly he turned around and started to move in the direction from which he had come. Then he stopped short.

"My starving people!" he cried. "I cannot return to them without food. What am I to do?"

For the first time since his departure from the ice palace, he remembered the advice the elf had given him. "In low places, use your feet." He was certainly in a low place – for his many tumbles had finally brought him to the base of the mountain on whose peak his ice palace stood. It would be best, therefore, to follow the elf's advice exactly.

He placed one foot ahead of the other, being careful to leave plenty of space for the long, wooden shoes. With each sliding step forward, he swung his shoulder and arm, bending a little for balance. Although his pace was very slow, he managed to keep on his feet. As he went along, deeper into the valley, he became more sure of himself. He found himself swinging along at a steady gait, and he began to go faster and faster. Then he was gliding over the slippery ground with such speed that snow flurries whirled around him.

"This is wonderful," he said aloud. "I couldn't be traveling more easily and swiftly! It's as if I were seated on the back of my faithful steed, Dark Storm, galloping over the countryside on a summer's day."

His spirits soared higher and higher. The white landscape flew past his delighted eyes. At this rate . . .

Then suddenly, bewildered and dismayed, he fought with the long wooden shoes and managed to stop himself just in time. Only a few feet ahead of him, rising straight up out of the snow, was a mountain. King Brynne lifted his head and stared upward, through the swirling snow.

"What now?" King Brynne asked himself. "It's useless to try to go around such a mountain. It would take too long. Besides, there are probably others like it on the way to the Southland. But how am I to climb such a wall? And on these clumsy shoes?"

And then King Brynne seemed to hear again the words of the elf: "In high places, use your head."

Ah, yes, he thought, that was the second piece of advice the elf

had given him. But what had he meant by it? It was different when he had advised, "In low places, use your feet." That had made sense. He had kept his feet firmly planted on the ground and had made splendid progress. But surely the elf couldn't mean for him to try to work his way up this steep mountainside on his *head* — somersault fashion?

"In high places, use your head," the good king muttered aloud.

Greatly perplexed, he stood looking at the forbidding mountain looming up before him. At first he saw only a few sharp rocks, sticking out here and there above the snow and the ice. But as he kept staring, he noticed a cluster of fir trees. Looking closer, he found that the mountainside was dotted with such clusters. Many of them were entirely buried in the snow, but some were not.

King Brynne uttered a glad cry. "Now I have it!"

He singled out a cluster of fir trees near him, which were taller than the others. Keeping his fur mittens on both hands, he started to clear away the snow from the roots and trunk of one of the trees. It was straight and sturdy. He tried to bend the trunk. It made a wide loop but as soon as he let go of it, it snapped back. He tried several more times with the same results.

"I can't even bend it, let alone break it from its root," he muttered, deeply disappointed.

But wait. His knife. With shaking fingers, he reached inside his fur robes. It was still there. He pulled it out and plunged it into the soft wood of the little tree's trunk. Mustering all the strength he had in his hands, King Brynne worked the sharp blade farther into the wood. Finally the trunk began to give way. Then King Brynne bent the tree and broke it off entirely from its stump.

"Now for another one the same size," he said. There were plenty to choose from. Soon he had selected the right one. This time he knew just what to do, and it was much easier bringing down the second tree than it had been the first one.

"I'll whittle the trees into poles." He cut all the branches off and stripped the trunk of bark. The result was two white, beautifully smooth poles. He grasped one in each hand and leaned heavily on them. They were strong enough to bear his weight.

"Now, Sir Elf, what do you think of King Brynne's using his head in steep places?" he exclaimed triumphantly.

He started confidently up the mountainside, sliding first with one foot and then the other just as he had done while crossing the level ground down in the valley. But for every step he took forward, he slid back two.

Perhaps if I turn the wooden shoes in like this, he thought, it will keep them from slipping.

But then they crossed, and he somersaulted backward, down the mountainside.

"These tumbles have brought me back down into the valley," he said in disgust. "But now I must climb out of it."

After trying first one thing and then another, at length he hit upon a sideways motion, turning the toes of the shoes out. With the help of the poles, he was able to keep the ground he had gained upward without any backsliding. The higher he went, the better he climbed. At last he swung himself up over the very top of the mountain.

"That was a real test of using one's head," King Brynne said breathlessly. "I doubt that a single king in the neighboring valleys would have been capable of doing it in a like situation."

He made his way over to the other side of the mountain peak. He looked down. There was an almost straight drop into the valley below. King Brynne began to feel dizzy. The surrounding mountain peaks whirled in circles about him. What was he to do next? The elf had given him no advice that would serve him here.

He peeked over the edge again. He was as frightened as he used to be when a little boy, trying to make himself dive into the Bry River. In those days, he would shut his eyes, count to three, and jump!

"You were young and limber then," he reminded himself, speaking aloud. "Besides, this is quite a different matter. Now you will have to take off from a mountaintop that is much higher than the bank above the Bry River. It is the dead of winter when everything is frozen solid. And you have a strange pair of wooden shoes dangling from your feet."

Yet King Brynne had not the slightest notion of turning back. He had only one thought in mind. At all costs, he must save his starving people. He would let nothing prevent him from continuing his journey to the Southland, however hopeless things might seem.

He made sure that the magic shoes were securely fastened to his

feet. He threw his shoulders back and took a deep breath. He placed his feet close together. Then he moved three steps nearer to the brink of the precipice. He crouched so low that his body almost touched his wooden shoes. He let himself go.

He felt himself gliding down over the slippery snow. He went faster and faster. Without any thought of what he was doing, he raised both arms in front of him. They began to swing with a rhythmic motion. His body had suddenly straightened. He was floating into space. He felt himself soaring like a bird through the air. He bent his head and looked down. Below him he could see white snow. Gradually his speed slackened. He let his knees bend as he landed on firm ground. His muscles relaxed. Now he was sliding gently downward on the soft snow. He came to a dead stop. He had reached the foot of the mountain.

Again King Brynne took a deep breath.

"Nothing but magic could have made me do this," he said aloud. "Thank you, Sir Elf."

Down on the level ground of the valley once more, the shoes were no longer a problem for King Brynne to manage. His feet slid into exactly the right places. As he glanced back, he saw neat, straight tracks in the snow over which he had passed.

"I am flying like a bird," King Brynne cried out joyfully. "Only my wings are on my feet instead of my shoulders."

He began to take an interest in the scenery through which he was gliding. It was beautiful with evergreens, whose branches, heavy with snow, drooped in sharp angles to the ground. For some time he followed the River Glommen. He was amazed to find that, where the current was swift, it was open. In Brydalen everything had been frozen hard when he left.

On the shores of Lake Mjosen, King Brynne came face to face with the first human being he had met on his journey. It was a fisherman carrying a large basket of fish.

"Good day," King Brynne called out when he was within hailing distance. "That is a fine catch of fish you have there."

The fisherman gave King Brynne one look. Then with a yell of horror, he ran away.

King Brynne was puzzled. After a little he understood. "It is the magic shoes that have frightened him. But how am I to buy food for my starving people, if everyone runs away from me? I must be very careful."

For his first call, King Brynne chose a farmhouse painted a cheerful red with white trimmings. Before starting up the lane, he hid the magic shoes behind a huge tree. A middle-aged man with a grizzled beard answered his knock.

"I came to ask if you had any grain to spare," King Brynne said, getting to the point of his errand at once.

"Why don't you plant your own grain?" the man asked.

"We have a famine in our kingdom!"

"That is the tale all beggars tell."

"I came to buy, not to beg."

"That is what they all say, too. Next you'll be telling me that your king sent you."

"I am the king."

For the first time the farmer looked at King Brynne enough to see his crown. He popped out of the door and seized King Brynne's hands. He bowed to the ground again and again. Then, turning to a woman with a baby in her arms and several tow-headed children clinging to her, he cried, "Here, Mother, and you children, don't you know a king when you see one? Even wearing his crown on his head!"

The farmer and the children went down to the granary with King Brynne. They filled sack after sack until King Brynne stopped them. "There are many mouths to feed here," he told the farmer. To himself, he added, "On my magic shoes I can go farther south and buy more grain."

The farmer and the children followed King Brynne down the lane. He stepped behind the tree where he had left the magic shoes, and strapped them on his feet. Then he looked back. The children were running toward the house. The farmer stood pale and trembling, his mouth wide open. "I have been dealing with an evil spirit," he yelled. And he started running after the children.

King Brynne chuckled as he glided over the slippery snow, his grain sacks bobbing merrily behind him. He was convinced now that he would be able to buy all the food he needed, and that the magic shoes would carry him safely back to Brydalen.

For a while he stopped to hide the magic shoes before knocking at the doors of the farmhouses. But as his chain of grain sacks grew longer, he became more confident. Soon he swooped down into the yards where the farm buildings stood, and waited for the people to recover from their fright before starting to bargain with them. Farther on, he rather enjoyed the cries of amazement that greeted him, and he even practiced fancy steps to impress those who were watching his approach. At last the magic shoes became so much a part of his journey that he forgot about them, and he ceased to pay any attention to the expressions of fear and wonder on the faces of those who beheld them for the first time.

Finally King Brynne said, "I shall go no farther. I shall turn north and go back to Brydalen."

But now a new difficulty faced him – one far more baffling than any he had met with so far. He had not been able to resist the full storehouses in the Southland, for he had thought of what all this food would mean to his starving people. Paying no heed to the size of the burden he was gathering, he had rushed on. To be sure, the tugging from behind had begun to make traveling on the magic shoes somewhat of a chore. But he had paid little attention to his aching muscles, telling himself that, after all, he had embarked on a very hard and long journey.

As he turned his face toward home and for the first time looked behind him, the sight that met his eyes struck him dumb. For as far as he could see, there were sacks and sacks and sacks.

"Why didn't I consider earlier how I was to take the food back to my people?" he moaned. "Over level ground here in the Southland, the pulling will be hard. Crossing the mountains farther north, it will be absolutely impossible."

The situation was too terrible for tears.

"I shall have to leave most of the sacks," he decided at last, still speaking aloud to himself. "But how am I to give food to some of my people and leave others to starve? If each person gets only a little, no one will be saved."

He gazed mournfully at the bulging sacks that trailed behind him. Then he straightened his shoulders.

"I shall have to take them," he said. "At least I shall do my best. On this journey, things have looked dark before. But whenever my need has been the greatest, help has been close at hand. I have faith that a way will be found now, too."

He took one step forward. Then another and another. The long shoes began to glide over the snow, and gradually the tugging from behind ceased. King Brynne went faster and faster over the level ground in the lowlands and then upward into the mountains. When he reached a peak that towered far above the clouds, he looked back. The sacks extended down the steep slope, across the valley, and up to the summit of the mountain he had left behind. Still keeping his gaze fixed upon the trailing sacks, he started down the slope ahead of him. The sacks bounced merrily forward as lightly as though they had been filled with air.

King Brynne was on the verge of tears. "This is magic," he said in an awed voice. Then lowering it to a whisper, he asked, "How can I ever thank you, Sir Elf?"

As he climbed mountain after mountain and crossed deep valleys, he began to plan how he should go about dividing the food among his people. The smallest children and the feeblest old people would have to be cared for first. After that, perhaps the ladies and the lords of the court. No, that wouldn't do. The people down in the valley would be just as hungry, if not more so. "I will leave it to Queen Edel. She will know better about such matters."

With this thought cheering him, he now began to think about how good it would be to find himself safe and comfortable in his ice palace once more. But then suddenly he realized that his home would never be the same without Prince Melchior, and all the joy of his homecoming was gone.

Pictures of Prince Melchior as he remembered him from bygone days kept running through King Brynne's mind: as a baby dressed in white bearskin, chasing rainbows where the light from the candles and the hearth struck rough surfaces on the ice walls. As a little boy, holding the mane of his father's favorite steed, Dark Storm, as he sat perched upon his back, and digging his small, brown fur shoes into the sides of the patient animal. And as the thoughtful older child on that memorable night of the elf's visit, willingly leaving parents and home in order to save the people of Brydalen.

As he thought about his son, King Brynne sobbed aloud. Immediately he was ashamed of his weakness. "Who am I to put my grief above the suffering of my people?"

King Brynne was now traveling so fast that he seemed to be leaping from one mountain peak to the next. He tried to sing. But the dreary notes that rose from his throat, no matter what tune he meant to sing, sounded like nothing but the weird whistling of the wind that swept over the barren white waste.

As he swung into the courtyard of his ice palace, Queen Edel stood there in the snow to welcome him. She made no effort to hide

either her laughter or her tears when King Brynne embraced and kissed her. The lords and ladies came streaming out of the ice palace. They surrounded King Brynne and bade him welcome. And he, in turn, took the hand of each one and thanked them all for their expressions of affection and loyalty. Some of the noblemen began to play on the flute and the harp. Others beat drums. The ladies of the court curtsied to him again and again, danced and sang for him. The servants came out, too, and many of them wept at the sight of their master.

"We must think of our people down in the valley," King Brynne called out loudly enough for all to hear above the tumult of his homecoming. "Prepare a feast immediately. Invite every man, woman, and child to come up here to the ice palace. No living creature in my kingdom shall go to bed hungry tonight. Later, Queen Edel will distribute the food according to the needs of all."

Queen Edel smiled. "Come, we must make haste," she told the lords and ladies and the servants.

Soon the welcome odors of cooking food began to drift out of the kitchen into the rest of the ice palace, and into the courtyard, and down into the valley. The people sniffed hungrily. Word traveled among them that there was to be a feast, and in no time they were all on their way up to King Brynne's mountaintop.

King Brynne and Queen Edel came out to the edge of the cliff to receive them. "Look," King Brynne said, pointing to the path over which their people were coming toward them. "This must be to honor the memory of Prince Melchior."

Queen Edel wept at what she saw. All the people carried evergreen boughs which they tossed over the white snow as they slowly made their way up the mountainside.

"Yes," she said, "it is for our son. They loved him very much."

Inside the ice palace, where tables were crowded into every inch of space in every room, more food was set out than the people of

Brydalen had ever seen all at one time. There were stewed mutton in cabbage, and meat balls, and roasted venison and grouse. There were sheets upon sheets of crisp flat bread with huge cubes of butter and cheese. And for dessert there were cream puddings and stewed berries and every variety of tart and cake imaginable. All the guests were given places on the long benches drawn up to the tables — men, women, and children — and they were told that they should eat to their hearts' content.

"Prince Melchior would have rejoiced with us, had he been here," King Brynne said in a low voice.

Queen Edel clasped his hand.

Then, without any warning, the lights in the palace went out. Everyone stopped eating. The smaller children, who had been swallowing their food faster than their elders could feed it to them, started to cry.

King Brynne opened his mouth to speak. But before he could say anything, the palace was flooded with lights — and these were even more dazzling than the lights had been on the night the strange elf had first appeared.

The children stopped crying. The grownups sat speechless. King Brynne gasped and Queen Edel held her breath. For between the high seats of the king and the queen, with his eyes sparkling, his cheeks glowing, and a smile on his lips, stood Prince Melchior.

"Prince Melchior!" Every one of the guests murmured in astonishment as they rose from their seats.

Suddenly there was such a tumult of joy inside the ice palace that the surrounding mountains rang with the echo of it. "Hail! Prince Melchior! Hail! Hail! Hail! Welcome home to Brydalen."

King Brynne and Queen Edel stepped down from their high seats, their faces radiant with happiness. Prince Melchior beamed first at his parents and then around at all the other people present at the feast.

"Thank you all," he said, "for the welcome you have given me. But it is really my friend, the elf from Trond Mountain, whom you should hail. He it was who sheltered me at his home inside Trond Mountain during my absence from Brydalen. He it also was who brought me safely back to you. And now," he went on, still smiling, "I have a surprise for you. A gift from the elf to every man and woman and child in my father's kingdom. My friend and the other elves living inside Trond Mountain made these gifts especially for you. They let me help, too. As soon as this feast is over, I shall present the gifts to you."

The children, in spite of their great hunger, could scarcely wait to see what it was that the elf had sent them. But their parents, who were curious too, coaxed them to finish the wonderful meal. When at last not even the hungriest growing boy was able to swallow another mouthful, King Brynne rose from his high seat once more.

"Prince Melchior wishes you all to come out into the courtyard," he said.

Urging each other along, all of the people crowded outside the ice palace. As they looked over the cliff and down into the valley and across to the white mountain opposite them, they were speechless at what they saw. Moving down the steep, white slope of the opposite mountain, across the lowland and up King Brynne's mountain, was a yellow streak. Catching the glow of the moon and the stars and the northern lights, it shone like a gigantic band of pure gold.

Prince Melchior pointed to the gleaming bar. "They are magic shoes that you see," he said. "Hundreds of them. A pair for every man and woman and child in Brydalen."

The people began to murmur and the murmuring rose to a shout of joy and laughter. King Brynne and Prince Melchior moved from one group to another, helping to fit the shoes and fasten them properly. The mountainside was covered with slipping, sliding, sprawling people, as each and every one of them tried to manage the strange, magic shoes. Laughter echoed across the valley.

No one in Brydalen, not even the smallest children, went to bed at all that night. And during the weeks that followed, the people could talk of nothing but the food their wonderful King Brynne had brought for them from the Southland, and the magic shoes the elf had sent by their beloved Prince Melchior.

After that first night, the older people, politely but firmly, refused to have anything more to do with the strange, long, wooden shoes. Secretly, among themselves, they termed them new-fangled notions and not fit for human beings. But most of the young people and all of the children kept trying until they had learned to use them.

"We can fly, we can fly!" they cried as they took off from high places near their homes.

Gradually King Brynne persuaded the older people to put on the magic shoes, too. "Look at your children," he told them. "Surely you do not want it said that you are not as clever as they." And once anyone had had the experience of jumping off a mountain peak and floating through space, nothing could make him return to the slow, tiresome walking of the old days.

One evening Prince Melchior asked his parents, "What are we going to call these shoes?"

"I hadn't thought of that," King Brynne admitted. "But it is true, they really should have a name."

"I know," Queen Edel exclaimed. "As I was standing out in the courtyard watching the young people and the children, it seemed to me that they looked like clouds floating in the sky. Why couldn't we call them *the cloud shoes?*"

"Not *skyskoene,*" Prince Melchior objected. "No one would take the trouble to say all that."

"Why not *skyene* then?" King Brynne asked.

"*Skyene* would mean the clouds," Queen Edel said.

"That's all right," King Brynne said. "One shoe could be called a *sky* – a cloud. Only I think we should change the spelling of the word *sky* to *ski*. Then the people would know when we were talking about the clouds and when we meant the wooden shoes. To make the exact difference between the two words clear from the start, I shall have this put into writing. I'll send out a royal proclamation and have it read to everyone in Brydalen."

"Does that mean that *ski* is a real word in our language now?" Prince Melchior asked wonderingly.

"It certainly does," King Brynne answered proudly. "And it will become a well-known word all over Norway some day. I shall invite the kings and princes of the neighboring valleys to come to see our skis. And with Prince Melchior's help, they will learn how to make some for their own people."

People say that if you happen to be in Brydalen on Christmas Eve and you stand on the mountaintop where King Brynne's ice palace used to be in the old days, you can see a strange yellow streak against the blue-white snow. It runs down the mountain of the ice palace, across the valley, and up to the opposite peak. And if you look carefully enough, you will see that this yellow streak is really a chain of hundreds of pairs of skis. But the stars must be shining and the northern lights flashing over the heavens and the moon must be out. Otherwise, you will see nothing at all. And usually the winter nights in Brydalen are still very long and exceedingly dark just as they were in those long-ago days.

The End.